Partners

Partners

by Deborah Shayne Syme

Illustrated by Jeffrey Wiener

UAHC Press • New York, New York

For Jane and Sid Shayne, my parents
For Josh, my son
and
For Danny, my husband and partner

Josh and Jacob are best friends.

They live next door to each other and go to the same school.

On Friday nights the two
friends go to the same
synagogue with their parents.
Last Shabbat, Rabbi Klein said something in her sermon
that they did not understand: "Every Jew is God's partner
in making the world a better place."

When they got home,
Josh and Jacob asked their parents,
"How can people be
partners with God?"

Josh's father wasn't sure.
Jacob's mother told him to
ask Rabbi Klein. When Josh
and Jacob saw each other at religious school,
they decided that they would ask Rabbi Klein
next Shabbat how they could help God.

On Friday morning, Josh's and Jacob's class went on a field trip to a museum in the city. It was very cold outside, so they put on their warmest coats, hats, and gloves before they got on the school bus.

As the bus got closer to the city, the children no longer saw beautiful homes with trees and flowers. Josh and Jacob saw only tall buildings and streets lined with cars and trucks.

Near the museum, the bus turned down a side street. Suddenly, Josh and Jacob sat up in their seats. They could not believe their eyes. They saw broken-down houses, with no glass in the windows. Broken furniture and trash covered the street.

JACK'S DELI

The people on the street looked
cold and unhappy. Two men without
coats slept in a doorway, under
cardboard boxes. An old woman dug
through a garbage can, searching for
something to eat.

At last, they reached the museum. Josh and Jacob ran to their teacher, Mrs. Silver, and asked her why those people were living in the street.

Mrs. Silver explained that they were very poor. Some had no jobs. Some had no homes. And all over the country many Americans went to sleep hungry.
"Why doesn't someone help them?" asked Josh.
"Why doesn't someone give them food?" joined Jacob.

"It's very sad," said Mrs. Silver, shaking her head. "The president helps a little. The mayor of the city helps a little. Churches and temples also help. But most people just don't care."

As their teacher walked away, Josh turned to Jacob and said, "I care. Do you?" "I care too!" answered Jacob. "Then let's do something!" yelled Josh.

For the rest of the day and all the way home on the bus, Josh and Jacob made plans. They hardly paid attention to anything inside the museum. They were too busy thinking of ways to help poor people. They made a list:

Give twenty-five cents from weekly
allowance money to a charity
organization.

Take two cans of food from home every week and drop them in the synagogue's "Feed the Hungry" food barrel.

16

Take old clothes to the neighborhood
thrift shop.

Give one new Chanukah or birthday
present each year to the hospital.

Run a backyard carnival and give the
money to tzedakah at religious school.

When the bus stopped in front of their houses, Josh and Jacob were so busy with their list that Mrs. Silver had to remind them to get off. They couldn't wait to tell their parents about the field trip. They spoke about their ideas all through the Shabbat meal.

"I'm very proud of you and Josh," said Josh's mother. "At synagogue tonight, why not tell Rabbi Klein about your plans. And don't forget to ask her your question about being God's partner."

Services seemed endless that night
for Josh and Jacob. After the
closing prayer, they burst out
of their seats and headed
for the social hall.

At the Oneg Shabbat, Rabbi Klein saw the two friends trying to get her attention. She invited them into her office and asked, "What's all the excitement about?" Josh and Jacob took turns telling her the story of their field trip and all the ways they planned to help the cold and hungry people.

"That's wonderful," said Rabbi Klein.
"You are two of God's littlest
partners."

"So that's what you meant in your sermon last Shabbat," said Jacob. "Exactly," answered Rabbi Klein. "You see," explained the rabbi, "God cannot make this a better place without our help. Every Jew can be God's partner in healing the world. We help to do it by making sure that every person has food and clothes and a place to live."

Josh and Jacob looked at each other. "We have a lot of work to do," said Jacob. "We sure do," said Josh. "God needs more partners." Then the two friends ran to find their parents. God needs big partners too.

About the Author

Deborah Shayne Syme, author of *The Jewish Home Detectives*, received her master's degree in Education from Wayne State University. She presently resides with her family in Stamford, Connecticut.

About the Artist

A graduate of Florida State University, Jeffrey Wiener is an illustrator living in New York City. His illustrations have been published in the *New York Times* and other national publications.